"Your Great Grandfather Henry, several times removed, was a lovely and brilliant man," Granny had said to her on that gloomy March afternoon, typical for England. "But rather than embrace his inner duality, he was fearful and ashamed of his licentious yearnings. A deadly combination. By attempting to bifurcate, and thus manipulate, his two inner selves, he created a formula that did far worse. He gave rise to the Beast."

"In Russ Colchamiro's YA thriller, the line between monster and hero blurs with every surprising twist. Packed with high-stakes intrigue and pulse-pounding action, HYDE AND SEEK: THE FURY OF THE WHITE MASK is monstrously fun!"

-**Sawney Hatton, author of DIRTY SPIRITS and EVERYONE IS A MOON**

__AGENTS OF THE ABYSS__

FRANKENSTEIN: MONSTERS OF THE ABYSS
STARING INTO THE ABYSS
MURDER AT CASTLE DRACULA
THE ABYSS STARES BACK
WOLVES OF THE ABYSS

Books by Russ Colchamiro

ANGELA HARDWICKE SERIES
CRACKLE AND FIRE
FRACTURED LIVES
HOT ASH
BLUNT FORCE RISING
TRIGGER POINT

OTHER WORKS BY RUSS COLCHAMIRO
CROSSLINE (SPACE OPERA)
MURDER IN MONTAGUE FALLS (MYSTERY/HORROR)

Padwolf 13 Series:
APOCALYPSE 13 Edited by Diane Raetz

MERMAIDS 13 Edited by John L. French

FANTASTIC FUTURES 13

Edited by Robert E Waters & James R Stratton

LUCKY 13 Edited by Edward J. McFadden III

CAMELOT 13 Edited by John L. French and Patrick Thomas

Other Anthologies from Padwolf
BAD COP NO DONUT Edited by John L. French
NEW BLOOD: Tales of Vampires
Edited by Diane Raetz and Patrick Thomas

Russ Colchamiro

Edited by Patrick Thomas and John L. French

PADWOLF PUBLISHING INC.

WWW.PADWOLF.COM

www.facebook.com/Padwolf

www.theagentsoftheabyss.com

HYDE AND SEEK:
The Fury of the White Mask
Written by Russ Colchamiro

edited by Patrick Thomas & John L. French

© 2025 Patrick Thomas

cover by Daniel Dragonov

Agents of the Abyss created by Patrick Thomas and
all related characters and settings are © and ^{TM} Patrick Thomas

ISBN978-1-958310-08-3

FIrst Printing.

To all who struggle with their inner Monster...

1

The poison dart sliced the crisp autumn air with deadly intent. Agatha arched her neck just in time to avoid the projectile, which otherwise would have punctured her carotid artery. Agatha was a spy, after all. And left unchecked, spies are always up to no good. Teenage spies are even more so.

Because teenage spies—spies in training, to be more precise—insist their short time on this mortal coil infuses them with all the wisdom they will ever need.

"You know you can't win, you mutated freakazoid," Agatha taunted as she contorted her small, petite frame into the very lethal weapon it was. Wearing flexible combat gear, she studied her opponents and their respective positions in the Winstar Forest. "Make your move. Go ahead. I dare you."

The existential threats teenage spies pose are further amplified when they also happen to be Monsters. Or, in Agatha's case, a teen spy who hails from a long bloodline of Monsters. One with a cellular capacity for strength and dominion she could not fully comprehend.

But her innermost powers and associated risks had not yet been activated within her; MI7 did not permit the descendants of Dr. Henry Jekyll to access the Hyde formula until they reached adulthood.

"Die, you evil wench," parried Lily Guepard. The genetically altered cheetah, who looked almost human, was perched behind a grey boulder. Tall, upright, and wearing a tech-enhanced nylon body suit, Lily sported cheetah timing, strength, reflexes, and physiology. She utilized those attributes brilliantly to blow another poisoned curare dart through a bamboo chute. The barb ricocheted off a giant sequoia tree in the dense forest, toward Lily's arm. "You can employ countermeasures until Mr. Beane untwists his face, but your luck, like this day, is over."

The smaller but no less deadly Agatha, with Olympic-level agility, leapt hands over feet into a cartwheel, then back-flipped through a thicket of leaves, scattering them into a camouflage swirl. With her blonde braid fastened securely down her back, Agatha landed in perfect position atop another boulder, opposite Lily.

Appearing as a dark, faceless shadow, with brilliant sunlight radiating behind her, Agatha momentarily blinded her attacker. "Nice try, you Dr. Moreau reject. Just because you purr like an overgrown alley cat doesn't mean you won't choke on a canary. Like this!"

With the strategic advantage of higher footing, Agatha whipped a metallic throwing star, which swerved around Lily. It pinged off another sequoia, pinning the Cheetah's tail to the ground.

"Now!" Agatha slid down the boulder, rolled across the dirt and leaves, and with fierce determination, leapt up and front-kicked Lily in the chest.

Under normal circumstances, the Cheetah, with her lean and lanky torso and whip-strong tail, would have brushed Agatha aside. But behind her legs was a lumpy force, neutralizing the feline's quickness and agility.

Because she was being held down by a young man who—unseen by the human eye—had ducked on the ground and wrapped his arms firmly around Lily's feet.

"Gilbert," Lily said, letting her guard down. "Come on. You may be invisible to everyone else, but thanks to my whiskers, you're as obvious as the staff Agatha's about to swing at my head."

"W-what?" the invisible teen stammered and, succumbing to his insecurities, instinctively studied his crotch. "No! I mean... it's cold out here!"

"Right," Lily said, and winked at Agatha. "That must be it. I can see it"—she tried to hold back a chortle—"all."

In addition to being invisible, Gilbert was also quite naked. He unclasped Lily's feet and covered up his unseen genitals. "No, you can't."

"You fall for it every time," Agatha said. "Gilbert. Of course, she can't see you. You're *invisible*. But either you need to get more comfortable with yourself... or start wearing clothes!"

"All right, young ones, all right," said Mr. Snow, a senior instructor at Dame Sanctum's Boarding School. The Gilded Age mansion, occupying a private estate on the northwestern outskirts of London, opened in 1052 during the First Age of Monsters. The school was rebuilt from scratch after the Great Fire. "That's enough for today."

Walking cane in hand and dressed in a navy-blue three-piece suit and gold monocle, Mr. Snow—a wise and disciplined Yeti—produced a handheld device. He deactivated the VR fight simulation, revealing the school's inner oak walls and ornate decoration.

Frustrated she hadn't been able to get the best of Lily, Agatha hadn't lost the contest. But she hadn't won either. Lily was her toughest challenge yet. If Agatha couldn't defeat the deadly cheetah during a training exercise, what chance would she stand when the stakes were legitimately life and death?

Agatha followed a long line of ancestors starting all the way back with Great Grandfather Henry Jekyll. But she hadn't been enrolled in the Dame School for spies as an academic exercise. For nearly a decade, starting at age five, she'd been trained in multiple forms of combat, espionage, intelligence, and counterintelligence to help save the world one mission, and one enemy, at a time.

"Agatha," Mr. Snow continued. "A letter came for you, but not with the regular post. It's regarding your gran. It appears we have a problem which requires our immediate attention, with implications that could shift the balance of power in ways we simply cannot allow." Mr. Snow's white Himalayan fur, trimmed close, tidy, and a touch provincial, seemed to turn a shade of grey, revealing a weariness to which the students were not accustomed. "You may have to enter the field far sooner than we thought."

2

The twenty-foot portrait of Mr. Snow loomed over Agatha and her friends, mounted on the wall behind his desk. But then, he was not a Yeti to be taken lightly.

Mr. Snow lit his pipe, the scent of warm orange and vanilla saturating his office. The cozy library was lined with leather-bound books only but a select few the world outside knew even existed. Most of the titles were worth killing for many times over. A Tibetan rug covered the length of his office.

Agatha's heart thundered as she leaned forward in the short chair in front of Mr. Snow's double pedestal executive desk. "Granny's *what?*"

"Kidnapped," Gilbert said. Utterly invisible, he appeared to them as an animated school uniform hovering in the next chair.

"Repeating the obvious is your go-to move," Lily said. Seated in the last of the three chairs, she had never fully embraced having an Invisible on the team. Then again, before Gilbert, no one had ever been born an Invisible. "But how, Mr. Snow? Why?"

"Yes," Agatha said. "Who did it? Is it…?" She stopped in mid-thought, transported to a place in her mind she had prayed would never see the light of day, but feared was inevitable.

"The Hyde formula," Mr. Snow said. "Her kidnappers know—or believe—your gran has access to it and are demanding it in exchange for her safe return."

Granny Sara had warned Agatha the Hyde formula might one day be leveraged as a bargaining chip against her. And if it did, Agatha would be called into action—forced into doing something unspeakable—whether she was ready for it or not.

"We are all of us in battle," Granny told Agatha on her thirteenth birthday.

"What battle?" Agatha had asked as they hunkered in the basement of Granny's cottage in Newcastle upon Tyne. The University city was perched in England's northeast, nearly equidistant between London to the south and Edinburgh to the north.

Granny pushed herself away from the washing machine. The heavy hunk of machinery covered a secret compartment beneath the slate flooring. "Against the deadliest enemy of all."

Just minutes earlier Agatha had been fretting that Liam Helmsford, an older lad from the Dame School upon whom she'd had a not-so-secret crush, didn't fancy her back. Which, as a result, would render her in a state of consternation not seen since the Dark Ages.

Yet Granny's words sent the handsome Liam, who had first caught Agatha's eye during his school performance as Macbeth, hurtling as far from her thoughts as the tiniest raindrop falling on the Thames.

Agatha may have only been a young teen then, but as a Jekyll descendant—whose parents had died years ago on a mission for MI7—she had been trained to push her anxieties aside when duty called. She'd made progress in that regard but still had work to do.

"Who, Granny?" Agatha trembled despite herself. She feared that, much like her parents before her, she had started down a life-altering path from which she might never return. "Who's our deadliest enemy?"

"One must only look in the mirror," Granny said.

Agatha had heard throughout her lifetime, from her parents and Granny herself, that each of us are our own worst enemies. Agatha had chalked that phrase up to cliché, something adults uttered to placate children when they didn't have concrete answers, nor the humility to admit such.

Then, however, in Granny's basement, Agatha felt a far deeper and more powerful meaning that dwelled within the recess of her warning.

"Me?" she said, never more aware of her body's enduring changes. Puberty is tortuous for even the most even-keeled teen. As the descendant of Monsters—with Hyde-altered Jekyll blood coursing through her veins— puberty was a physical, emotional, and psychosexual metamorphosis few would ever truly understand. "*I'm* the enemy?"

Granny chuckled, though her countenance turned

serious. The well-known MI5 was the British Secret Service division focused on domestic threats, MI6 with international conflicts. MI7, however, was comprised largely of Monster-trained spies who dealt with Monster threats. Top secret and highly classified, the very existence of MI7 would be denied by all involved.

"We are all in a never-ending battle between the dark and the light—within ourselves. Every sinner craves to be a saint or, at the very least, to be perceived as such. Every saint lusts to be a sinner. You, my dear, as am I, are both sinner and saint. Hero and villain. Liberator and captor. We are caught between virtue and vice, love and hate, peace and violence. Don't waste your breaths protesting what cannot be refuted. You will need every wisp of air your lungs can sustain."

Agatha knew Granny's words to be the truth, even if she didn't quite understand why.

"Your Great Grandfather Henry, several times removed, was a lovely and brilliant man," Granny had said to her on that gloomy March afternoon, typical for England. "But rather than embrace his inner duality, he was fearful and ashamed of his licentious yearnings. A deadly combination. By attempting to bifurcate, and thus manipulate, his two inner selves, he created a formula that did far worse. He gave rise to the Beast. It is only through years of genetic research and some crafty refinement of the formula that we, the Jekyll/Hyde bloodline, can absorb its properties and withstand its deadly effects. Anyone outside the bloodline who takes the formula will go mad within three days and perish from it. But during those three days"—Agatha felt the terror behind Granny's narrowed eyes—"it will be a world filled not just with sin, but unchecked power and unspeakable horror. Do not run from your inner Beast, Agatha. Make peace with it. Embrace it. Embrace her. Or she will overtake, and finally, destroy you."

3

Back from her daydream, Agatha studied Mr. Snow as he produced a thumb drive, inserting it into his laptop computer. Projected in the center of his office was a 3D image. A video started, showcasing a single head, covered in a white mask, with red vibrating eyes.

"We have Sara Jekyll, Dame School alumnus, MI7 agent, Monster, and grandmother to Agatha Jekyll," a distorted voice said. "Deliver the Hyde formula in forty-eight hours, or we will experiment upon Grandma Jekyll until she becomes, even in Monster form, unrecognizable."

The video intercut to Granny chained to a chair, blindfolded, blood dripping from her nose—no small accomplishment given that Granny was one of the most lethal Jekylls alive. Her inner Hyde took things to a whole new level. So Agatha couldn't understand why Gran didn't transform. Until they saw something around her neck.

"She's stuck in the same kind of MI7 explosive metal collar they use on werecreatures," Lily said. "If she transforms while wearing it and grows too large in the neck… it'll blow. Must be how they got Granny. If she goes full-on Beast, it'll kill her."

"Indeed," Mr. Snow said. Lily's heart thundered with fear. But she had to smother it.

"As you can see on her face," the voice continued, "we have already begun." The video zoomed onto Granny's left hand. The middle finger had been severed at the knuckle, another impressive accomplishment, one requiring the means and know-how to execute. "As for her finger… you should have received that as well."

Mr. Snow unwrapped his handkerchief.

"That's Granny's ring!" Agatha's adrenaline spiked so intensely she wanted to murder Granny's kidnappers with her bare hands. With strength she'd amplified through the rigorous and sometimes excruciating training regimen the Dame School had put her through over the last decade, she could have.

The white-masked voice continued. "Send a message to the email address at the end of this video. In the subject line, in all caps, type the words 'I UNDERSTAND.' We will contact you with instructions about where to make the exchange."

The image of Granny disappeared, so that only the white mask was visible. Its red eyes seemed to beam even darker. "To make the exchange, send the granddaughter, Agatha Jekyll," the voice commanded. "Grandma Jekyll has already told us much about your operations. About your team of Monsters. Who knows what she still has to say?"

The video cut to black, with only four words in bold, block letters left in the center screen: ***BEWARE THE WHITE MASK.***

"Anyone able to blackmail us over the Hyde formula would never return Granny for it," Lily said. Her tail flipped back and forth with anxious precision. "Never."

"Agreed," Mr. Snow said. "The global stage is ever more deadly, although, in truth, it would be imprudent to suggest, much less state outright, that it has ever been a safe, gentle, or kind world."

"No!" invisible Gil said, his shirt tie bouncing up and down nervously. "They can't! Not Granny!"

"We have to save her," Agatha insisted. Just shy of sixteen years old, she spoke from a place of dread—and humiliation—as she was still a decade too young from being approved for the Hyde alchemy herself. "But the formula. It's so… dangerous."

"Indeed, it is," Mr. Snow said. "But the formula is only one element of our conundrum. First, the kidnappers knew of Granny to begin with. Second, they knew her location, and how to find her. Three, they were able to subdue Granny, despite her mastery over the Hyde power and the ability to transform almost instantaneously. Four, they knew how to contact us without being traced, which means they know far more about us and our operations than we know about them, and more than we would ever permit. And five... we cannot retrieve a sample of the Hyde formula from MI7. We must assume we are compromised and cannot risk further exposure. We must handle Granny's private sample. She has her own supply. Despite it being unsanctioned."

"Which means we have something those wankers want," Lily said, the savage stalker in her revealed through her yellow, feline eyes. "So we're still in the game. And to some extent, have leverage over them."

"Too right," Mr. Snow said.

Agatha, who could barely breathe, thought about Granny and all she'd learned from her, and the conversation they'd had years before, in case something ever went tragically wrong. Like now. Agatha gazed upon the Yeti, and the layers of consternation set deep within his white fur face.

"Mr. Snow," she said, calling upon her inner determination. "It's time to read the letter."

The Yeti sat motionless. He breathed uneasily.

To Agatha, the silence was louder than a football match at Wembley Stadium.

If read aloud, Granny's words, whatever they might be, could expose secrets, and reveal a potential risk, far beyond what they'd been trained for. A risk they had to take.

It was Granny, after all.

Mr. Snow leaned forward in his chair. It creaked, as if expressing the tension they felt but dared not acknowledge.

"I had long hoped this day would never come." His black, manicured claws extended from his white fur hand and rested on the desk blotter. "But I have it here." He handed over the brown envelope, addressed to Agatha, and sealed with a dollop of maroon wax. He handed Agatha a brass letter opener.

Agatha studied the envelope. She considered the consequences. Then sliced it open. Inside was a parchment, with a note written in quill ink. It said:

"Agatha-
The family lives
The family dies.
But do not succumb to thieves and lies.
Jekyll by day
Hyde by night.
Take a sip and hold it tight.
Journey to Wiltshire
Where our secrets kept
Tho pour one out lest ye never slept."

"Lest she never slept?" invisible Gil said. "Are you off your trolley?"

Mr. Snow and Lily studied Agatha, who looked up from the letter, with a wry smile on her face.

"I know where to find the Hyde formula," she said. "Wiltshire's the key."

"She hid it at Stonehenge?" Lily said. "The tourist trap? Oh, bollocks to that, mate. Tell me Granny isn't as daft as that?"

"No." Agatha shot eye daggers at Lily for the obnoxious insult about Granny. "Not daft at all. Yes, it's at Stonehenge. But not in Wiltshire."

"Forgive my confusion," Mr. Snow said impatiently. "But where?"

Agatha stood up from the chair. "A piece of piss. It's at the other one."

4

Agatha was deep in thought the entire train ride to Liverpool. The maritime city in the northwest quadrant of England had fallen on hard times, stemming from its own downturn, amplified by the Great Recession that began in America in 2008. Although in recent years Liverpool found itself making an economic comeback.

A week earlier she had fretted about her upcoming sixteenth birthday, and if it would be a celebration worth remembering, including a good, juicy snog.

But now, the thought of a boy's lips on hers seemed childish and foolhardy, the musings of a selfish, petulant twit.

Mr. Snow had outlined a plan for the team that would challenge them far beyond what they'd ever faced. Nevertheless, Agatha reviewed the plan until she could recite it, down to the last detail, at the drop of a hat. And yet she still wasn't sure if she could pull it off.

Granny Sara was more than just her grandmother, her mum's mum. After Agatha's parents died, she lived with Granny during Dame School breaks, under the roof of a woman who had seen and done more in one lifetime than most villagers do in a century.

Through necessity, love, and loyalty, Granny had

taken on the role of Agatha's parent, teacher, mentor, friend—and drill sergeant.

From the Liverpool Central train station, Agatha and her crew walked under the cover of dusk over to Ryley's Gardens. The wrap-around street was just far enough away that the locals could disappear into their favorite watering holes for the night and enjoy a pint or five with their mates. All without having to deal with the constant flow of tourists who wanted to pile into the Cavern Club and other Beatles-themed attractions which, for better or worse, pumped copious funds into the local economy.

"The formula's in here?" said the invisible teen. As a nervous habit, he was chomping on a piece of gum. To the unsuspecting eye, the pink wad appeared to be bobbing up and down in the air of its own accord. "Seriously?"

Agatha hadn't been to the pub since she was a wee lass. Being back now, with a team she wasn't sold on to be effective in the field, twisted her guts. But nostalgia won the moment. Even if prepared for an internal tug of war, the pull of the past can outweigh the urgency of the moment.

"Granny always told me that unless I was careful, my future was here," she said, not the least bit surprised Granny had had the foresight to envision a scenario such as this one so many years in advance. But that was Granny, so much more than ever met the eye. "I never realized what she meant. I do now."

Lily's cheetah instincts swelled. She spoke with more than a hint of derision. "You realize, of course, the name of the pub is The Stone *Hedge*, not Stone*henge*."

"Yes, thanks much for cracking that code," Agatha said. "It was an old joke between us. It's my Uncle Jack's place. When I was little, I saw a photo." She produced it. Agatha and Granny were standing out front, with the sign in full view. "I kept saying Stone*henge* because... you know."

"And that became a thing."

Though confined by her outfit—flexible combat pants and top, and a brown leather vest with various pockets—Lily's tail flicked to and fro, an anxious habit she had before jumping into a mission.

"Yes," Agatha said. "It became a thing."

"So what are we waiting for?" Gilbert spit out the gum. The pink wad shot through the air and into a trash bin. "Who fancies a pint?"

"Nice try," Agatha said. "You know the rules. No clothes, no service."

"Awww," Gilbert pouted. "No fair. Besides... who'll know? I'm invisible."

Lily leaned forward, placing her hands on the ground, and arched her back—a full feline stretch—tempting Gilbert to check out her taught, shapely bum. She liked taunting him, mostly because it was fun.

"Will be kinda obvious," she purred. "A pint'll float in the air then vanish down your gullet."

"I can pull it off," Gilbert said. "I've got wicked skills! There's more to me than my body, ya know? I have a mind."

Agatha rolled her eyes. "Don't be a twat. But I'll make you a deal. We get the Hyde formula and Gran back safe and sound… you'll get your pint."

"Seriously? Really?"

Agatha smiled at Lily. "Sure. You with a pint? I'd pay to see that."

Banter aside, Agatha was gutted about Granny and what her predicament meant for them both.

Like all Jekylls who chose the Monster path, Granny had taken the Hyde formula—as an adult—allowing her to transform into the Beast that lurked deep within the Jekyll bloodline. Yet thanks to considerable MI7 and Dame School training, she was able to control her physical metamorphosis into the Beast, and the urges to rampage, murder, rape… and worse.

The Hyde strength and power were at full force in Hyde mode. Even when Granny held her 'normal' human form, her strength was considerable. Although it was far more freeing—and satisfying—to go full-on Beast.

It was strictly forbidden, however, to take the Hyde formula before one's 18th birthday, and rarely approved for anyone younger than 25. By then, the frontal cortex of the human brain has typically approached, if not reached full maturation.

Agatha and crew waited to enter the pub until the sky was pitch black, once the locals had gotten into their groove.

"Oi! Agatha!" they heard, greeted by a dimly lit pub half-filled with customers. "That you?"

"Hey, Uncle Jack."

"Great to you see, Luv," he called from behind the bar. "But whatcha doin' all the way up in Liverpool?"

Agatha deftly scanned the pub, assessing the layout. She did her best to sound casual. In control.

"Time for our first pint, mate. Pour me one?"

But what she wanted, badly, almost desperately, was to leap over the bar and jump into his arms like she did, back when she was small enough for him to hold, feeling the warmth of his chest. The cocoon of safety.

To be nothing more than what she should have been, would have been, had her life even remotely resembled anyone else's her age—a teenaged niece, seeking solace and comfort from a relative who had done nothing but love her since the day she was born.

For her uncle, an adult, to take the reins of responsibility. To take the pressure away. To fix the problem. And bring her gran back home.

But being a Monster—and a spy—rendered that impossible.

This was her mess, her *assignment*. It was time to stand tall.

There was a delay before Uncle Jack's eyes drew tight beneath raised eyebrows. He took a short breath, immediately recognizing their pre-arranged code words for just such a situation.

"Oi! Mates!" He rang the copper bell above the bar, getting everyone's attention. "Sorry, folks, sorry. Gotta close early."

"Oh, whaddya on about, Jackie?" one of the locals whined. "Pour us another, gov'ner."

"Love to, Maggie. Love to. But I got someplace to be. All right, off ya go."

Despite protests and groans, Uncle Jack cleared the pub within ten minutes. With the last of his customers gone, he bolted the arched wooded door from the inside, closing on its black metal hinges.

"Aggie. You're so big," Uncle Jack said, giving her a proper hug. "Who's your mate? She's very, um... exotic."

"Uncle Jack... Lily. Lily... Uncle Jack."

Lily extended her five-fingered hand, replete with feline knuckles, pads, and claws.

"That's some grip," Uncle Jack said, shaking out his hand.

Lily grinned, her yellow eyes studying him. "And I haven't started to play."

"And that's...," Agatha said. "Oi! Gilbert! Put that back!"

The glass door to the mini fridge behind the bar seemed to open of its own accord. A bottle of Newcastle Brown Ale floated in the air. The bottle cap popped off.

"What the...?" Uncle Jack said.

With her feline agility, Lily hopped atop the bar, snatched away the beer bottle and, from a dish near the serving station on the bar, tossed tequila salt on Gilbert's face, partially revealing his shape.

Uncle Jack shuddered, then blinked slowly. "So, uh... Aggie. This is yer team, yeah?"

"Yep. And we don't have much time." Agatha explained their predicament.

Her eyes aglow, her teeth sharp, Lily was on the prowl—and ready to strike. "So, where's the formula?"

"That's just it," Uncle Jack said. "I don't rightly know.

It was for my protection. It's here... somewhere. Only Gran knows."

Agatha studied the pub's interior—the columns, tables, wood crossbeams, ornamented molding, framed photos, light fixtures, and the bar itself, including five brass taps. "I know where it is."

"*You do?*" the others said in unison. "*Where?*"

Agatha recited the letter again.

"The family lives
The family dies.
But do not succumb to thieves and lies.
Jekyll by day
Hyde by night.
Take a sip and hold it tight.
Journey to Wiltshire
Where our secrets kept
Tho pour one out lest ye never slept."

"Take a sip. Pour," Agatha said. "I think it's in the taps. In the handles."

"The taps?" Uncle Jack said. "Oh, come on, luv. We've been pouring from those taps for twenty bloody years. I woulda noticed if the formula was hidin' there. There's no bloody way it's..."

Agatha could see the doubt, then recognition, come alive behind Uncle Jack's eyes. For nearly two decades he'd been a guardian, inches from the family secret, without being aware of it. He was one of the few Jekylls in their family line who had chosen not to take the formula.

There was also the three percent to consider—a subset of Jekylls whose DNA rejected the formula, with lethal results. Uncle Jack wasn't in the three percent. He simply did not want the Monster life—or responsibility. But he supported the cause.

"The taps." He shook his head and chuckled.

"What?" Agatha said.

"When we first bought the pub, Gran brings me a present, yeah? She said every great pub needs a set of great taps. She gave me the tap handles." Music themed, they were hand-carved in the shapes of an electric guitar, acoustic guitar, stand-up bass, string of piano keys, and a saxophone. "She said, no matter if I'm having a good night or total shite, all I had to do was pour a pint and think of her, and all would be well. The cheeky old bird."

Uncle Jack turned off the interior lights, a half-moon leaking in through the stained-glass windows. He stepped behind the bar and reached beneath the countertop. He moved aside three pint glasses. With his middle finger, he pressed a button on the underside of the bar.

Flecks of tequila salt gave definition to two fingers and half of Gilbert's palm. "I'll get it." He reached for the first tap.

"No!" Uncle Jack warned as he reached out his hand, although it was just an instinctive gesture, too far away to make any difference. "I haven't—"

Gilbert tugged on the tap handle. An electric shock sent him hurtling across the pub, smashing him into the jukebox. "Ain't That a Shame" by Fats Domino kicked on.

"Gilbert?" Agatha inquired.

"I'm okay," he mumbled, his salted head leaning against the jukebox. "All good."

"I have to switch on the safety," Uncle Jack said and did so beneath the bar. "The only way to find the formula, wherever it is, can be found by activating the defense grid and working around it. The great paradox. That was Gran's idea. It's booby-trapped, mate. There are almost definitely more. I thought you knew."

"Well," Agatha said. "We do now."

Granny's security mechanism had ignited a grid of green laser sensors. The laser beams crosshatched throughout the pub.

Agatha recalled the course she'd taken on applied sciences. "What happens if we cross the beams?"

Uncle Jack cleared everyone from the bar area. From ten feet away, he tossed a pint glass through the air. Upon contact with the first beam, the glass vaporized, leaving a cloud of dust.

Agatha recoiled, not just from the exploding glass, but from a longing she couldn't ignore. The Hyde formula was close. She could feel it, a presence saturating her cells, a yearning more powerful than sexual desire.

The Beast lurking deep within her soul *had* to have it—a thrumming, savage biological need reaching back to the distant forces from the earliest days of Creation itself.

"I can do it." Lily's genetically manipulated eyesight, reflexes, and coordination enabled her to pre-cog the aerial acrobatics necessary to dance around the laser grid.

Agatha took Lily by the arm. The urges pulsed in her veins like a tribal drumbeat. "Don't. There's got to be a better way. We need to shut it down."

She turned to Uncle Jack, looking for the answer.

"Sorry, luv. This is Gran's doing. I've got no bloody idea how to disable the system. I'm not even sure we can."

Agatha felt the pressure to succeed and the fear of failure, overwhelmed by the urgency to complete her task. Granny's life—and the domino effect that would surely follow—literally hung in the balance.

Agatha gripped her hands into fists. In her mind's eye she recalled a single detail from her room in Granny's house—an orange and brown quilt they'd knitted together that one winter after she'd broken her ankle attempting, and failing, to pull off a double axel at the skating pond.

The Hyde power may have been her destiny, but that was a long way off. Instead, youthful overconfidence had blinded her to the realities that her strength and agility—heightened thanks to a decade of intense MI7 training—required a more sophisticated understanding of how each physical contortion impacted her strong but still vulnerable muscles, tendons, joints, and spine. In short, she was only human. She bled. Her bones still broke.

Concentrating on that quilt took Agatha out of her momentary anxiety, enabling her to focus again on the task at hand. Calmer, she caught her reflection in a wall-mounted mirror with a Bella beer logo stenciled on the glass.

"I have an idea." She pulled the mirror off the wall and, holding it up with both hands, angled the mirror between two laser beams. "Count it. One, two, three"— Agatha felt the mirror vibrate under the laser beam's pressure—"four, five..."

Lily leapt, knocking Agatha safely to the floor before the mirror did, in fact, vaporize.

Breathing heavily, Agatha was nose-to-nose with Lily. "Cheers. We've got five seconds. Let's go again."

They huddled, discussed a plan of action, then reset their positions. Agatha used another mirror to deflect the beams just long enough for Lily to twist herself through the green lasers and cat-leap over the bar, just before the glass shattered.

"Well done," Uncle Jack said.

Gilbert had a question. "Hey, uh, Uncle Jack. I want to check something. How do we get into the cellar?"

Uncle Jack looked at Agatha, who shrugged.

"It's in back, mate. But the quickest way... there's a trapdoor on the floor on the other side of the bar."

"Cheers," said Gilbert, whose partial outline disappeared. "Back in a tick."

"Uncle Jack," Agatha said, recalling long-forgotten details of her youth, "you remember Christmas with Granny? All the music she played?"

"How could I forget? Bit of a rock n' roll goddess, she was, back in the day. Hung out with all the legends. Hendrix, Bowie, the Stones, The Kinks, The Moody Blues. The stories she had." Uncle Jack broke out in a smile. "Aggie... what was that one song she used to love? The Beatles' tune? Offa *Let it Be*."

"'Two of Us,'" Agatha said, her mind drawing deeper into the song.

"Yeah! That's the one! She loved that one line about...

shite, what was it?"

"Can't totally remember," Agatha said. "But there's definitely a bit about burning matches and lifting latches."

"Yeah. Burning matches," he said as his eyes drifted to the glass bowl of matchbooks on the bar. "Lifting latch... es."

Agatha and Uncle Jack shared the same realization. "*Lift the latches,*" they said together.

"The taps," Lily inferred. "We have to lift the taps!"

"But he pulls on the taps a thousand times a day," Agatha said. "How can that...?"

"There's another switch," Uncle Jack said. "Under the bar. Gran said I'd know what it was for when the time came. She said, 'it's just the two of us, luv.' Had no idea what she meant at the time."

"So, you flip the switch, then we pull the taps," Lily said. The edge of a moonbeam glistened off her whiskers. But unbeknownst to her, the tip of her tail grazed a pint glass, at the edge of the bar. It teetered back and forth.

The three of them held their collective breath, terrified the pint glass would fall into another laser beam which, if redirected, could kill any one of them.

Though only three feet separated Lily from the pint glass, it might as well have been three thousand kilometers. Even with her genetically enhanced feline strength and reflexes, there was no way for her to reach it in time. Nor was she in position to pivot and snag the pint glass, if it indeed fell, without running through the laser grid.

Still holding their breath, they tried to will the pint glass to settle back on the edge of the bar. It ticked a millimeter toward the edge, then back, then toward the edge once more.

And then, finally, the pint glass—effectively, a hand grenade—seemed to settle in place.

"Oh, thank the bloody luck," Uncle Jack said, exhaling a breath of terror and relief they all shared. "That could've been bloody awf—"

The glass tipped over, dropping toward the floor.

Before they could react, the pint glass fell into a low-angled laser, ricocheting the beam such that it changed trajectory, a shard of the pint's shattered glass slicing through Uncle Jack's left kneecap.

"Christ!" he cried and dropped forward, blood spurting from his leg. "Aggie."

Heart in her throat, Agatha tore the bottom off Uncle Jack's shirt and quick-twisted it into a tourniquet.

"Ah, Christ! Not so tight!"

"Sorry, mate. But we have to stop the bleeding."

"Your gonna stop my bloody heart!"

Agatha had to ignore Uncle Jack's pain, knowing how desperately she needed to retrieve the Hyde formula, and do so before he bled out. "Lily," she said. "You're up."

"Uncle Jack," the Cheetah said. "You okay, mate? Where's the other switch?"

"It's there." He grimaced, gripping his knee. "Two steps to the left." Lily encroached and extended her arm, nearly hitting another laser. "No. Sorry. *Don't* move," he warned sternly. "*My* left, my left. Sorry-sorry. Your *right*. Move to your right."

As if she could shoot laser beams of her own from

her yellow eyes, Lily scowled at Uncle Jack, but let it go. No time for that now. Instead, she exhaled, turned her head slowly, then side-stepped into position. She ducked down and, utilizing her extraordinary feline eyesight, found the switch underneath the bar.

"Agatha. I'm gonna flip the switch, alright?"

Agatha looked to Uncle Jack who, despite his pain, nodded in the affirmative. "Do it."

Lily did, then stood up. "Unless you tell me not to, I'm gonna open the taps."

Nearly shaking beneath the remarkable pressure of the moment—Agatha had led several simulated missions at the Dame School, but never in the field—she nevertheless found her poise. She nearly said yes, when she realized something critical.

"Wait! We can't have beer spilling all over the place. We need to contain it."

"Bloody hell," Lily said. "I didn't even think of that."

She deftly produced five individual pint glasses from behind the bar, then aligned them side by side beneath the taps, which were not in line with the laser beams.

"Okay, then." Lily put one hand each on the first two taps, everyone wincing as she did, almost expecting the pub to explode. "Here... I..... go." She pulled on the taps, beer flowing into the pint glasses, with no ill effects. Lily continued with the last three taps.

Agatha exhaled with a smile. "That was bloody close. I was really worried there for a—"

"Uh, mates," said Gilbert, who had returned from the cellar. "Bit of a cock up."

Lily flipped up each of the five taps, shutting off the flow of beer. "What?"

"What the hell?" wailed one of Uncle Jack's customers, staring drunkenly at the portions of Gilbert's naked body defined by tequila salt. "Jackie? What is this unholy creature? Am I dreamin' or am I just pissed as a fart? He's… I mean, he's…"

"Arnold!" Uncle Jack said, fighting through the pain in his knee. "You musta passed out in back again. This is just… uh… listen, mate. You're on the piss. There's nothin' to…"

But reacting as one does to the site of a semi-visible invisible teen and a cheetah/human hybrid, Arnold stumbled back into a beam, the laser slicing his head clean off. His torso hit the floor with a *thud*, followed by his severed head, with a *squish*. It rolled at Uncle Jack's feet. Both eyes were open, staring up at him.

"Oh, sweet Jesus!" Uncle Jack said. "I'm gonna be sick."

Agatha had seen corpses before, training in the morgue, but never one she'd been responsible for. And in this case, due to sloppy work. It was standard MI7 protocol to clear the space before you engage. She didn't kill the man herself, yet in failing to do her job as team leader, the result was the same. "I just… I'm…"

Uncle Jack chundered, the vomit splattering on poor Arnold's face. "This is why I never took the formula or joined MI7. I'm not cut out for this load of bollocks. Just… oh, Christ. Cover him up, please. Just do what you came for."

Knowing an apology was a sad and hollow gesture, Agatha let her silence convey all that needed to be expressed. She'd caused the death of an innocent man. Something she'd have to live with forever. She eased Arnold's severed, vomit-covered head away and draped it with a jumper someone had left behind.

"Well, that was awkward," Gilbert said. "You'd think he never glimpsed an invisible bloke before. Anyway, don't know what you did up here, but there's Semtex lining the cellar underneath the bar. The timer kicked in. If the counter on Granny's bomb is accurate, we have"— he glanced at the wall-mounted clock—"nine minutes and seventeen seconds to get the bloody hell outta here."

"What?" Agatha recoiled. "But how? What did we"— she thought then about the lyrics to the song—"do?"

She blinked repeatedly, humming the song to herself. "Burning matches, lifting latches... Burning matches, lifting latches... Burning matches, lifting... *lifting!* Lifting latches. We have to lift!"

"Lift?' Lily said. "What do you mean lift? I lifted!"

"Lily. Clear the bar. Get fresh pint glasses. Quickly but, you know… not too fast."

"Quick but not too fast?!"

"J-just," Agatha stammered. "I dunno. Be careful!"

Lily removed the full pint glasses, careful not to spill any beer. Then, finding large plastic pitchers that could hold more liquid, she positioned them on the serving trough, one each beneath the taps.

"The song," Agatha said. "Two of Us. *Two.* It's a two-person job. Show Gilbert where the switch is." Lily did.

"Gilbert. Take hold of the switch. But *don't* flip it. Not yet. Not until I say. You hear me? Don't. Bloody. Move."

"Got it," he said from behind the bar.

"Now, listen. Everyone. Uncle Jack… I'm gonna lift you up. Can you manage?"

"I'll have to," he said, leaning his arm on her shoulder.

"Lily," Agatha continued. "When I say so, you're gonna open all five taps again. Let the beer flow, with the taps pointed down. Then… *only* when I give the signal… you're gonna close all five taps, lifting them up. You hear me? Not one at a time, but all at once. Run your arm along the front of the tap handles so you can lift all five latches in one motion. Understand?"

Lily nodded.

"Good. Now… Gilbert… flip that switch off, you hear me? It's okay. Do it now."

"You sure?"

If ever in her short life Agatha wanted to be sure, needed to be sure, it was then. But she wasn't sure. She was *almost* sure. Hopeful. But with only minutes to go before the pub exploded, she had no time to debate. So, as leaders do, she asserted her surety, even though it was nothing more than assumption.

"Yes. I'm sure."

Gilbert flipped the switch.

"Well done," Agatha said. "Lily… don't do it yet, but when I say 'one, two, three now'… you lift the five taps at once. And Gilbert, *at the same exact time*, you flip that switch back *on*. But… you both make your moves when I say the word 'now,' and not before. Got it?"

"Got it," Lily said.

"Hunky dunky," Gilbert said.

Agatha took a final deep breath, exhaled. "Okay. Here we go. Lily. Open the taps. Let the beer flow into the pitchers." She did. With the ale flowing, Agatha initiated the next critical phase. "Okay, mates. One... two... three............ *now*!"

In one motion Lily flipped the five taps back up—cutting off the flow of beer—as Gilbert flipped the switch beneath the bar.

Just an inch from Lily's hypersensitive whiskers was the copper bell Uncle Jack had rung earlier. On a mechanical track, a small panel to which the bell was secured shifted aside. It revealed a small cut-out within the vertical support beam behind the bar.

Fastened within an apparatus were three glass vials, each containing red bubbling liquid.

"Whoa," Gilbert said. "Is that...?"

"The Hyde formula," Agatha said, almost licking her lips. "Too bloody right."

Like a vampire aching for an open vein, she nearly ran through the laser grid to take hold of the exotic elixir that had changed her bloodline—and family history—forever. The need nearly overcame her senses. The struggle was real.

"Agatha," Gilbert warned, "we've only got another minute."

Agatha shook herself back into focus. "Lily! Grab the vials!"

Lily snatched the Hyde formula and secured them

into a leather zip pouch with a specially sectioned interior that could withstand any pressure short of an alien invasion. She pulled Gilbert by his invisible scruff and, powered by their survival instincts, they all scrambled, avoiding the laser grid, out into the cold, pitch-black night.

They had run as far as they could into the alley when The Stone Hedge, Uncle Jack's place of business—his refuge from the world of Monsters—exploded. The blast tossed them down the cobblestone street, smoke and fire mushrooming over Liverpool.

"Uncle Jack." Agatha stared into the inferno, her face covered in soot, trying, but failing, to express the depth of her remorse. "I'm sorry, mate. I'm really sorry."

On his bum, gripping his wounded knee, Uncle Jack watched his life's investment go up in cinders. Orange flames crackled against the Liverpool night. "Yeah. Me, too."

"I'll give you one thing." Ash gave Gilbert's body definition in places he would have preferred remained a mystery. "You sure know how to plan a road trip. At least we have something to bargain with."

Maybe," Agatha said, shaking. Not just because she was out of breath, which she was, but because of what she was about to do, as much as she knew she oughtn't do it.

She snagged the zip pouch from Lily and, despite being an unsanctioned move, told herself she was taking the fight to the enemy. But there was no denying she was motivated by an uncontrollable craving to, once and for all, access the nearly demonic power lurking in the recess of her soul. She shook the vial. The red liquid turned a dark purple.

"Agatha!" Lily cried, the roaring inferno radiating immense heat. "What are you doing? We need that for—"

Too late. Agatha opened the vial. An eruption of vapor escaped as she drank the Hyde formula, finally embracing who she was always meant to be, if only a few years earlier than intended.

Such that as her new self, the Beast rising in the dark Liverpool night, surrounded by roaring flame, it was clear to all that Agatha's life—and her destiny—would never be the same.

5

The Hyde formula took effect instantly. Her petite body began to mutate, bubble, and grow, from a teenaged human into something far more alchemic, potent—and deadly.

She stood eight feet tall—the largest Hyde ever known—with outsized muscles and mass, weighing more than 30 stone. A scalding volcano of destruction and madness erupted in her veins with uncontrollable ferocity.

Confused by a permanent reorganization of her DNA, Agatha had a nearly unquenchable need to rip the spine out of an alligator and feast on its entrails... or whoever happened to be within her now considerable reach.

Lily, sooted Gil, and Uncle Jack were not her compatriots, but corrosive maggots, rabid animals in need of torture—and extermination.

"Yes," Agatha growled, marveling at her size, strength… and power. "Yes. YES!"

"Ag… Agatha," Lily quivered. "What in the hell…?"

"No, not Agatha." The psychotic Beast in her instinctively dominated Agatha, who had been utterly unprepared for this second persona, much less for its tyrannical, unhinged savagery. "Blythe. And Blythe wants to play."

And it wasn't that Blythe simply *wanted* to maul them like a serial killer obsessing over her first prey. She hungered for the stalking, the hunting… the butchering of life… simply because she willed it so. Nothing but intense, grotesque violence would satiate her unquenchable bloodlust.

No! Agatha screamed, locked in the cage of Blythe's tormented mind. *What are you doing? Don't!*

Silence! Blythe snarled in their shared mind, leaving Agatha's comrades only able to see the demented look in the Beast's eyes. *What a feast before me.*

No! Those are my friends! My family! You can't!

Friends? Family? What a pathetic fool you are. They are savory slabs of walking meat. The only question is… which will be most succulent? The thighs? The forearms? The guts splashed out? Where should I start?

And to wash it all down? Their blood. Their salty, crimson blood. A city of lambs asleep in their beds, begging for slaughter. To violate in the most heinous ways, and to hear them scream—yes, the screams!—as I rip them apart. One organ at a time.

What kind of Monster are you? Agatha rebelled. But she was overwhelmed by the sheer magnitude of Blythe's psychotic savagery.

The kind that bathes in their horror as I dismembered them—their helpless knowing. It will be most… satisfying.

Lily stood in a fighting pose, although going into battle with the newfound Beast was far from ideal. "Agatha! Remember yourself."

"There is no Agatha. Only Blythe. And Blythe wants

to kill you."

"No," Lily demanded. "You have to fight it. You are Agatha Jekyll. Daughter of Theo and Amelia Jekyll. Granddaughter of Sara Jekyll, descendant of Doctor Henry Jekyll. You are a member of the Dame School, a provisional agent with MI7. We are your allies, your comrades. And your friends."

Buried deep within the Beast, Agatha heard Lily's muffled plea for sanity. But as the dominant personality now, all Blythe could see—all she could feel—was a mongrel in need of slaughter.

"Remember why we're here," Gilbert said, and while he may have been invisible to the human eye, Blythe saw his heat signature as clearly as the roaring flames behind him. "We have to rescue Gran. You remember. Gran!"

About to eviscerate the insolent creature, flashes blinked in Blythe's mind, as Agatha cut through the deranged Beast's inner howls. Granny. Dame School. Mr. Snow. A flickering image at dusk, of her mum and dad, chasing after her with giggles in Fulshum Park.

Agatha, indeed, was fighting back.

You have the power of the Beast, she said internally, clawing her way out of the foul-smelling cavern of Blythe's tormented mind. *But I will* not *become a Monster.*

Stop! Blythe shouted back. *This is my body,* my *life. You are the enemy. Because I am Blythe. I am powerful. And I… am finally… free!*

Agatha buckled beneath the sheer magnitude of Blythe's will. But she'd been trained as a warrior. Only now that battlefield was her own soul. Losing it to Blythe would not only be a fate worse than death itself—to become an uncontrollable agent of rage, torment, and destruction—but a permanent mark that Granny had failed her, and that she had failed Granny. And that was something Agatha could not permit.

I gave you that freedom, Agatha said. *I unleashed that power. It was a mistake, and one I'll have to live with. But remember this… as quickly as I gave you life… I can take it all away.* A bluff. *So let… me… GO!*

Never! Blythe howled. *There* is *no Agatha. There* is *no release! There is only Blythe!*

Blythe! Agatha shouted. Struggling against the mighty force trying to dominate her, she thought about Granny and the lessons she'd learned from her. *You will listen to me, Blythe, and you will listen to me now.*

No, I—

BLYTHE! Agatha shouted once more, only this time Blythe heard her. Feared her, even. But Agatha knew this could not simply be a battle of wills. She was a spy, after all, trained to manipulate her way out of trouble. *You have the bloodlust, the cravings. I know you do. I can feel them too. They linger on your lips and call to your very soul.*

They don't… Blythe protested but fell into the trap Agatha had laid before her, tempting the savage Beast with the very cravings she most desired. *Yes,* Blythe admitted… *they do.*

Agatha could feel Blythe's enormous heartbeat thud just a pulse slower.

You think you're free, Blythe, that you're the one on the prowl. But you, Agatha said, *are the hunted.*

Never! Blythe *is the hunter! Blythe takes what she—!*

Blythe has power, Agatha said, ignoring the Beast's protests. *Blythe has force. But Blythe is alone. You do* not *control your bloodlust. Your bloodlust controls* you. *Which means you are* not *in charge. You are a slave, serving another master, one you cannot see, cannot change and… no matter what you do… can never escape.*

How dare you insult Blythe! I'm *in charge! I make the rules. Blythe does what she wants!*

Really? Agatha taunted, realizing the way to Blythe was her ego, not her strength. *Is that so? You do what the* Master *wants. The Master in your soul* wants *you to feed, the Master* wants *you to kill. And if you do not obey… if you fight the Master… if you disobey… the Master will fight* you. *And that, dear Blythe, is a fight you will lose.*

What… no! There is *no Master. There* is *no… is there?*

It was at that moment Agatha knew she'd found her way out. Now it was time to lead.

Can you feel the call? Agatha asked.

No, Blythe said, instinctively, but was unable to resist. *Yes. I do.*

Can you feel the need?

Yes.

Can you resist the taste of blood?

Blythe could not lie. *No.*

Then I will take you there. I will lead you to the slaughter. And when Blythe is needed most… I promise to set you free. And when that happens… you will do what must be done… and feed.

Blythe reached a massive, hairy hand to their Monster

face, tormented by the two selves battling for control of one body.

Catching her reflection in the side-view mirror of a parked Mini Cooper, Blythe stared at the Beast staring back at her. But more so, in her tormented mind, she saw Agatha staring at her as she stared at Agatha, confronted with the duality of a self she could not escape.

Confused by Agatha's love and pain, two minds battling for dominance, the visage before Blythe was a grotesque, distorted version of them both, neither entirely human nor entirely Beast. Each half had laid dormant within the other, imprisoned, a nightmare of unsettled personalities waiting to be unleashed upon the world, fueled by an addictive form of demonic insanity, fighting against an inner humanity, tortured by it all.

Blythe howled into the night, picked up the car with both hands. And, with strength that seemed to feed off her fury, she tossed it across the street, smashing the vehicle into the dreary brick building. Concrete chunks and broken glass crashed to the street.

Yet it wasn't until she smelled the blood, Uncle Jack's blood, leaking from his wounded knee, did the human Agatha within truly appreciate the Monster that Blythe actually was.

"Aggie," Uncle Jack said, his body weakened and in distress. "Come on, mate. It's me. Uncle Jack. The Beast is a part of you, but it doesn't control you. You've been trained for this at school. And by your gran. Don't fight the Beast. Or the Beast will fight you back."

Their breaths heaving, Blythe and Agatha battled

each other to make sense of the noise screaming in their shared mind, including where they were, what they were doing, and how they'd even gotten there.

Yet as Agatha exerted more dominance, she became horrified at her hideous, chemically altered body, questioning her very existence, her life force insisting it be heard.

Am I a girl? A woman? A human?

Am I a Monster? An unholy creature?

Am I all those things? Or something else altogether?

Still trapped in the Beast's body, Agatha held her hands out—what she remembered as small hands with dexterous fingers but had morphed into massive, hairy appendages that could crush a man's skull as easily as a sour grape.

"N-no," she grumbled as the dirty secret slithered out from her soul. "No, no, no, no, no, no, NO!" The Beast fell to her knees, Agatha wailing at her transformation, then recalled a training session from just a few months earlier.

6

"**M**iss Jekyll," said Mr. Snow, back at the Dame School. "As was inscribed on the Temple of Delphi centuries ago, 'know thyself.' It means that one must embrace their abilities, accept their responsibilities, yet work within their limitations. Despite best laid plans, field conditions do not always conform to your wishes. When they do not, you conform to them."

Agatha hadn't appreciated then what Mr. Snow was trying to tell her. "You're not being fair," she'd protested. "My parents were killed on a mission. But you don't care. You're forcing me to grow up without them. As a spy! I don't understand what you want from me. It's too much."

"To live according to your nature," he continued, slapping her protests aside, "one must first acknowledge that very nature, rail against it, and in time, accept it, for all that it is and will be. Do not complain to me about what you do not possess or what you deem unfair. Assess, adjust, and decide. Because if you do not, others will do it for you, as they see fit, and according to their own agendas. And if that happens, your fate will be sealed, no matter how skilled you may one day become. Know thyself, Miss Jekyll, or your truest self—the one lurking deep within—will be a greater threat to you than all the world's enemies combined."

"Wait," the Beast growled, though it was Agatha's voice in the Liverpool alley. Uncle Jack's pub was burning to the ground. "Wait." Her breaths heaved, though partly by design, forcing their way through the thick protective lining of her Monster lungs.

Agatha could feel her organic identity claw its way through the debris of her reformulated psyche until, finally, she locked Blythe back in the cellar of their combatting soul.

Shocking the others and herself, the Beast's hulking body shuddered, then reduced back to Agatha's normal state. She looked at her reflection in a puddle in the street, her countenance again the Agatha Jekyll she'd looked upon until just moments earlier.

Her two selves had gone into battle—Agatha versus Blythe, human versus Beast. Against all odds, Agatha, her human half, had emerged as the victor.

"Blimey," Uncle Jack said. "That's..."

Her own dualistic sensibilities heightened, Lily wanted to believe the danger had passed. That her friend and fellow spy had returned, if not to normal, then to some close approximation. "Agatha. You okay?"

Although adrenaline and the Hyde formula were still whisking through her body as if they were trying to outrun the Apocalypse, Agatha was at least well enough to respond. "No," she said. "I'm pretty bloody far from okay. But also... yes. I'm..." She flexed her fingers in and out of a fist, ensuring she was in control of her newly enhanced body.

"Oi!" Gilbert said. "The car? The one you chucked. Can you do it again?"

Agatha looked at the demolished vehicle and considered his question. There was only one way to find out.

Stronger than she'd ever been in human form, although unable now to access her Monster power, Agatha grabbed the car's back bumper. She felt the vehicle move, lifting it several inches out of the rubble.

"Oi," she said, struggling with the car. "A little help?"

The others grabbed the car, and together they were able to pull it free.

"You're stronger," Lily said. "Much stronger. But not like the Beast."

"No," Agatha said. "Not like the Beast. But enough about me. We have to make the call."

From her burner phone, Agatha dialed the number she'd been given. It rang twice before someone answered.

Disguised through a digital program, the voice sounded as if a computer itself was talking to her. "Do you have it?"

"It's right here," she said.

A text came through with an address, in London's West End. Then another text. "*THREE HOURS. DELAY AT YOUR OWN RISK.*"

"Three hours?" Agatha said into the phone. "I don't think we can—"

The phone went dead.

Agatha took in the damage she'd inflicted on the streetscape, including Uncle Jack's pub, which was now a pile of falling timber and charred rubble. Police and firefighter sirens wailed in the near distance.

"Uncle Jack," she said with as much ease as she could muster, then texted Mr. Snow via her encrypted private mobile phone. "Ambulance is on the way. Speaking of which... I hate to ask, but... I need a favor?" She puckered her face into her best teen pout, hoping to ease the blow. "It's for Gran."

"I luv ya, Aggie. But you killed my regular, sliced open my leg, transformed into an actual Monster and back again before my bleedin' eyes, and destroyed my pub. It wasn't just the place where I worked. I bought it with my own money. We made a go of it, not perfect... even shite half the time... but it was my place. Twenty-three years... gone cuz of you and your mates. I know it's for Gran, and I accepted the risk before you were born."

"I'm sorry, Uncle Jack. I don't know what to say."

"Say? Bollocks to that. Don't say a bloody thing. Just get the job done. Find Gran, get her back safe, and take out the wanker who snatched her up. You do that... I can live with it. I'll heal. I'll get the insurance money. I'll rebuild. And I'm billing that damn school of yours for pain and suffering. But don't make me do it for nothin'. That, luv.... that would just break my bloody heart."

With Blythe lurking deep in her soul, rattling on the bars of its cage, Agatha knew Uncle Jack was spot on. All her training, all she'd learned, would be for a hill of shite if she didn't use it all to maximum effect when it mattered most.

"If we're gonna save Gran," she said, the fire blazing

behind them, "we need to be better. *I* have to. Because if we're not, I'm not sure how I'll ever be able to live with myself. Blythe is raging within me. She's howling to escape, every second. It's taking all my energy to keep her in check. And there's a nutter out there who won't stop with Gran to get the formula. To get to our drop I need your car."

Uncle Jack dropped his chin, then reached for his keys. He sighed. "Why the hell not? You've bollocksed everything else I own."

Agatha kissed him on the side of his cheek not covered in blood and soot. "Thanks, mate. I'll bring it back in one piece."

Uncle Jack eyed the three of them. "Damn straight, you will. Now go get Gran. She'll be pissed if you don't."

7

Lily drove them back to London beneath a hazy midnight sky, the three Monsters conserving their energy as much as was possible under the circumstances.

Yet as exhausting as their night had already been, it had not truly begun.

Knowing they would have to improvise in real-time, they confirmed through Mr. Snow that the address they were given was an abandoned garment wholesaler, and a likely White Mask checkpoint from where they would receive new instructions.

Which made it virtually impossible to establish a tactical plan. But no matter.

Agatha may have begun the assignment as a junior spy in training, untested in the field. Because now she was an entirely new Agatha—having unleashed, confronted, and dominated her inner Beast—with powers she could call upon as easily as she could whistle.

"Agatha," Gilbert whispered from the back seat. He was somehow more defined as a spicy beef pizza disappeared down his otherwise invisible gullet. "I know you didn't sign up for this, mate. Not really. But if it means anything, I'd never've been able to handle this as well as you have."

She nodded without looking back.

No, not well, she thought. *Not even close. I'm losing it. I'm afraid. Of what I'll do. And what I won't.*

Self-pity and terror may have reared their ugly heads, but Agatha needed to focus. Instead she ruminated over the directives they'd been given by Mr. Snow. He'd impressed upon them the utmost necessity to rely on their training, particularly regarding counterintelligence. They would need to lie with the practiced skill of the most devious con artists, rendering their enemies unable to know the difference.

And if they made it back to the Dame School alive, there would be consequences for her transgressions. Taking the Hyde formula without authorization and under MI7 supervision was one of the most sacrosanct provisions governing Monster operations.

The fear of reprisal, however, was the least of Agatha's concerns.

She studied the road in the black of night, easier than she had anticipated thanks to her enhanced vision.

The question she fretted over most was whether she'd activated her newfound abilities in time. Anyone dangerous enough to kidnap and overpower Granny without triggering her Hyde transformation, with intimate knowledge of MI7 and the Dame School, posed more than a calculated risk. It implied an inside job. And if that was the case, Agatha had to consider that at least one of her enemies, as much as she dreaded to entertain the idea, was riding along with her in the car.

I can kill them all, Blythe whispered in the recess of her mind. *Rip them into morsels and lick their bones clean.*

Oh, how succulent. How utterly... perfect.

The thought made Agatha shudder. The voice was loud. Seductive.

Her team—her friends—had no idea about the awful thoughts swirling in her mind, or the precarious position they were in. If Agatha were to slip, to let her guard down, even for a minute, Blythe would escape. To slaughter them all. And relish every moment.

But rather than respond to the Beast lurking within her soul, Agatha drove deeper into the night.

8

They arrived at nearly 3 a.m. down a dark alley. The confined narrow space in London's West End reeked of vomit, defecation, and soggy, days-old rubbish. The brick walls were tagged with various graffiti, 'FOR LET' signs, worn concert posters, and various nooks—ideal hiding spots for pimps, thugs, drug addicts, dealers, and stalkers alike.

"We're here," Gilbert said. "Now what?"

It's time for Blythe to feed, Blythe said in their shared mind, with more force than earlier. *You don't need them. You don't need anyone. Only me. I can smell their fear. Let me rip this city apart and find Granny Sara. I'll eviscerate anyone who gets in my way. And even if they don't.*

Yield! Agatha said. *Not yet.*

When?

Soon, Blythe. Soon.

Or we can do it now.

"There could…" Agatha focused on her breathing to control Blythe. If unleashed in Beast form, she was more than ready to employ her bare Beast hands and razor-sharp claws, ideal for ripping the viscera out of living bodies.

But they heard the low buzz of a mobile phone.

In response, Lily leapt to a windowsill perch, above

the steel windowless door. Taped behind a graffitied board was a burner phone. She dropped the device into Agatha's human-sized hands, a form she was struggling to maintain against Blythe's desires.

LOOK UP, a text read. She did. There, above the door, was a black security camera, in an alley where one would not reasonably expect to find surveillance apparatus. Agatha stared into the lens, which panned the alley.

Another text came through: *ACROSS STREET. 37. KNOCK ON DOOR.*

Agatha complied. Her crew at the ready, they were greeted with two short buzzes when the heavyweight door, also grey steel, unlocked with a metal *wronk*.

She led them inside the small, squat building. To the left was a short staircase up to the next level, though the entrance was blocked by a metal cross-hatched gate with laser shielding, reinforced locks, and another security camera. To the right was another door. A third text came through. *BASEMENT. COME DOWN.*

Still adjusting to the battle raging within, Agatha breathed deeply through her nostrils. She inhaled a spectrum of blistering scents she felt like a thousand daggers had pierced the various lobes within her Monster brain.

MI7 had trained her to suppress her fears and anxieties, to fold them neatly like a sweater and put them in a drawer. They have no place in the field. Except anxiety doesn't work that way. It shows up whenever it wants to, injecting a persistent thudding into your chest, disrupting your breath. Whether through meditation, medication, or other forms of distraction, how you deal with it is up to you. But you do have to manage it, one way or another

Perceiving Agatha's distress, Lily stepped up, putting her Cheetah senses to work. Sweat, urine, saliva, adrenaline. Salt and vinegar crips. Gurgling bile, in gastric reflux. "Four," she said. "There's four of 'em down there. And perfume. Autumn Rose."

"Granny's favorite," Agatha said. "She must be there, too."

As they came to the bottom of the dingy staircase, they saw, across the sparse industrial basement, Granny secured to a chair with a reinforced zip-tie. Her head was slumped forward.

"Look," Lily whispered. "They've still got her in the explosive collar."

"Yeah," Agatha said, her human heart pounding as the light from a single desk lamp shone on the side of Granny's face. From an overhead pipe, water dripped nearby, one slow, echoing drop at a time, into a puddle on the moldy, concrete floor.

Surrounding Granny were three thugs holding customized shotguns, one man and two women by their physique, standing upright and wearing white masks.

Unleash me, Blythe said. *Unleash me now.*

In her mind, Agatha saw the vision Blythe projected, where in one motion, in full Beast form, she would bound psychotically across the room and kill the three guards—fist to the throat, side kick to the sternum, and toss the third against the concrete wall, crushing her skull.

How easy it would be, Blythe said, drooling over the violently lecherous thought. *How satisfying. To stand over their battered bodies and taste the crimson platelets leaking from their veins.*

Staring at Granny, shackled like a rabid dog, Agatha was almost—almost—tempted to let Blythe do as she desperately craved. But Agatha knew this rescue, for now, required finesse, not rage. Nuance, not demolition.

She also knew that whoever had gone to such great lengths to kidnap Granny and hold her for ransom—in exchange for the Hyde formula—would never allow a rescue so easy.

"Agatha," said a young man who, from the shadows, entered the light. In beige slacks, white turtleneck sweater, and black wool sailor's jacket, he walked toward Granny with a deliberate gait. "I hoped you'd come. You look different since I last saw you. You're almost a woman now. Almost a full agent. I guess you stuck it out. Then again, you were always a believer, but never in the right ideas."

"L-Liam?" Agatha eked in a very un-Monsterish high and squeaky prattle. "Is… is that you?"

"Cheers," said Liam Calloway, who stepped deeper into the desk light's plume. The bulb illuminated a face Agatha had obsessed over more so than she wanted to acknowledge. Only it was sturdier now, more chiseled and defined. Yet beneath the polish was a depth of conviction one engenders having fought for his place despite being told unceremoniously and often that he is unwanted. Unworthy. Rotten to the core. He was seventeen the last time she'd seen him, nearly twenty-one now, taller than

Agatha remembered, his trim physique more man than boy. "So, you do remember. I thought you'd forgotten. We never did have a proper goodbye. Then again, we never said a proper hello." He smirked. "Not, at least, the way you wanted."

"What are you doing?" Agatha asked. "*Why* are you doing it?"

"Don't bother," Lily said. "You know what he wants. It's why he washed out of Dame School. He never cared about MI7, England, or anyone else. He was always after the formula. You remember. He always said, 'You have to be a Monster to fight a monster. Because monsters rule the world.' The conspiracy nutter to end all nutters."

"Take the *formula?*" Agatha said. "How? You can't do that. It'll kill you unless you're a ..." It was then that years of memory fragments, stray thoughts, and seemingly disparate conversations she'd overheard, including whispers of an illegitimate relative, coalesced into one reality. "You're not a *Calloway*, are you? You're... you're a Jekyll."

Liam offered a smug bow. "From a different line of the family. Pleased to finally meet you, dear cousin. I was, indeed, born Liam Calloway. But my mother was pushed out of the Jekyll family for marrying a free-thinking man. One who, like her, rejected the very notion that to take the Hyde formula, a descendant must hand one's freedom—and life—over to MI7. She was born a Jekyll but was henceforth known as Calloway. Like mother, like son."

"Bollocks," Lily said, her claws ready to strike. "MI7 would never have taken you in like that. They knew who you were."

"Of course," Liam said with a self-satisfied grin. "But under the provision that I kept my heritage a secret. They were grooming me, and others like me, for a special task force." He paced the floor like a University professor pontificating across a lecture hall. "An elite group who would do the agency's nastiest bidding. The kind one never chats about over a pack of bickies."

Agatha's every impulse—Beast and human alike— rejected his claims like an alley cat regurgitating an *e. coli*-infected rat. As she'd been trained to do, she watched the pulse in his neck. It never faltered. He was, as heinous as it was to accept, telling the truth.

"My mother surrendered the option to take the Hyde formula herself but would not have me denied my birthright. Like you, dear cousin, I have family blood coursing through my veins. But unlike you, I was one of the impure, never allowed to publicly embrace my heritage. Not, that is, until now."

In the time it took her to process even a single breath, years of hormones, intuition, and furtive glances revealed to Agatha what had been there all along.

"The Theatre Troupe," she said, fighting against Blythe's inner howls to transform, her heart beating like a stampede of wild stallions. "They told us it was an ensemble used to penetrate the arts, to recruit and surveille. But it was code, wasn't it? You were all training for black ops, right under our noses."

"At last we are having the same conversation." Liam's smirk turned nasty. "But after years of training to become their most lethal spy, learning to say, feel, and, of course, commit truly diabolical acts on their behalf, they said I couldn't handle the Hyde formula. That I'd never be ready."

"But why? If you're already in the bloodline?"

"Because," Liam said, "I'm in the three percent." He ran a hand over Granny's slumped shoulders, then nodded to the White Mask guards. "I have the genetic marker that renders my DNA incompatible with the formula. Were it to merge with my cells, it would kill me quickly and in a rather unpleasant fashion."

"Ohhh," Agatha said, strangely relieved. "*That's* why you washed out."

"I didn't wash out!" Liam backhanded Agatha across the face. Only her jaw didn't budge. Unprepared for the nearly cast-iron durability of Agatha's jaw, Liam shook out his hand. "But you, dear cousin, you *have* taken the formula, haven't you? *Tt-tt-tt.* As I figured you would, if you ever got the chance. Then again," he said, and licked his lips, "at heart, you were always a naughty little minx. You pretend to live in the light, but like me, you are drawn to the dark."

Staring at Granny, who had been reduced to a drooling, anesthetized victim, Agatha felt her inner restraint crumble, allowing Blythe, at long last, to finally have her turn.

Blythe? Agatha said.

Is it time?

Bloody too right. It's time.

Agatha finally gave in to her desire. To be ugly. And bad.

She let her body instantly morph into the Beast she'd been desperately waiting to unleash. Her size doubled, her appearance grotesque, her massive body raging with hatred, bloodlust, and power. For a deviant instant, Blythe was the dominant personality, seconds from committing extraordinary violence. Agatha wrestled it back.

Even in Beast mode, it was a battle of wills as to whose personality was in control—Agatha or Blythe.

"DON'T YOU…!" Agatha growled. But before she could rip Liam in half, three of his White Mask guards shoved their modified shotguns under Granny's slumped chin.

"Ah-ah-ah," Liam chided deliciously. "I wouldn't if I were you. Your gran might have taken the Hyde formula, but we pumped her with enough Rhino tranquilizer to take down a herd before she transformed. In her drugged-out state, her human state, I doubt the tranqs would have any trouble ripping holes in her face."

Agatha was right on the edge. She knew that unleashing Hyde would feel so wickedly good and satisfying, but the consequences could easily spiral out of control. Full of wrath, she threw her Beast fists into the wall. Chunks of concrete smashed to the floor. Exposing sharp, saliva-soaked fangs, she heaved and howled—a deafening roar.

Yes! Blythe goaded. *Don't talk. Don't reason. Just kill.*

Don't confuse me, Agatha said within her mind. *It's too delicate, too dangerous.*

But you want to, Blythe said. *Don't you?*

Like a recovering heroin addict staring at a fresh set

of works, Agatha hated herself for admitting it, but: *Yes,* she said. *I want to. I really do.* And she nearly did.

But gazing upon Granny with Beast eyes, and the precarious position they were all in, Agatha regained her poise. She obstructed Blythe, reducing herself back to human form. Though still possessing a modicum of the Hyde strength.

"Temper, temper, cousin. Being a Beast is one thing. Being a Beast in control of herself and with the discipline to harness those powers is quite another. So now we know you're an easy mark, let's get on it with it, shall we?" Liam gestured with his head. "You. Kitty cat."

"Lily," Lily said defiantly. "With claws sharp enough to kill your entire bloodline."

"Lily. Whatever pleases your fragile psyche. Who's got it? You… or Agatha? Who's got the formula?"

"I do." Lily reached into a side pocket in her leather vest. "It's right"—she winked at Agatha—"here!"

Lily leapt straight up, extended her claws, and, in one surgically precise move, knocked all three guns away from Granny's captors. She slashed the first White Mask guard, who recoiled into the second. Then, by the barrel, Lily swung one of the dropped shotguns counterclockwise, knocking the guard in the jaw with the chestnut stock, shattering his jaw and eye socket.

Agatha Beasted up again and grabbed Liam by the throat, his feet dangling three feet off the floor. "Don't underestimate me again."

"Oh," he grinned, though he could barely speak—or breathe. Her hot, acidic breath was pungent in Liam's face. "I never did."

Three additional White Mask guards rushed in from behind them, jabbing Agatha in the kidneys with batons. Electric currents dropped her to the concrete floor, leaving her, despite her Beast size and strength, in spasms.

"We use these on elephants," Liam wheezed. Standing again, he clutched his throat. "My focus in animal physiology has paid dividends. I wasn't suh-certain three would be enough. Let's make sure."

He nodded to the guards, who hit Agatha again and again as she howled in pain, reduced again to human form.

I told you! Blythe scolded Agatha. *Let me out! Let… me… KILL!*

N-no, Agatha pushed back, struggling to maintain control over Blythe, much less her consciousness. *Not yet.*

With acrobatic grace, Lily jump-flipped through the air to strike once more. Before she landed, Liam removed a pistol from his waist band and shot her in the foot, dropping Lily next to Agatha.

"I'm actually impressed," Liam said. "That was a bloody fine maneuver. You almost had me. But then, I know your moves, better than you know yourselves. You always thought I was aloof, but really, I was watching you. All of you. Always studying, always waiting, to finally make *my* move. I just didn't think it would take so long."

He nodded at the White Mask thugs, who patted Agatha down. "Here," the first thug said, removing the glass vile. The red liquid bubbled as if it was an imprisoned creature smashing against its cage, dead-set on its freedom. The thug handed it to Liam.

Eyes wide, Liam accepted the vial with the reverence one takes Communion from Christ himself, if only Liam believed in such things.

"In all my dreams, I never really thought this moment would come. It is quite a thing to obsess over your birthright—your destiny. It is very much another to have that moment actually come true."

Liam held up the formula to the dim light, mesmerized by the crimson liquid—and the power it could unlock.

"You," he said to the second thug. "Do the test. Make sure it's the Hyde formula… and that they haven't tampered with it. That's an MI7 classic. They are masterful at masking agents. They have a knack for it."

Agatha struggled to breathe. "How can you take the formula if your body will reject it? It'll kill you."

"Hmm, yes. It would. If I were really in the three percent."

"What?" Agatha queried. "But you said you were…"

Liam paced again, walking around them in a circular pattern. "No," he clarified. "*They* said I was in the three percent. Mr. Snow. But as the Dame School often does… they lied. They never told you about the Hydes, either, now did they?"

Agatha and her crew offered blank stares.

"No," Liam said smugly. "I thought not. Just as there are Jekylls, there are Hydes. Oh, yes. We're out there too. And believe me… we are far less docile than any Jekyll I've ever seen. But all in good time. You won't need to find the Hydes. They'll find you."

"They didn't… kick him out of Dame School because he couldn't take the formula," said Granny, barely conscious. "They suh-sent him as far away from it as possible, because of how desperately he wanted it. They were afraid of what *his* Beast might do, because they doubted they could control him. We thought it best if you didn't know."

Much like the two personalities in her mind struggling for dominance, Agatha was of two minds about Granny—swelling with love and relief she was still alive, yet awash with wounded teen pride at the secrets Granny had kept from her. But spies don't have the luxury of wallowing in that field.

"Speaking of not knowing." Liam jabbed the baton, seemingly into empty space. What he'd actually done, however, was drop Gilbert to the floor. Blood dripped from his otherwise invisible nose, revealing his partial upper lip. Liam pointed to his own eye. "Coded infrared contact lens attuned to the Invisible's specific condition. Took three years and ten million pounds to perfect, with some tech I… borrowed… from MI7. I've been watching him all along. I knew you'd hold him back, thinking I'd be unaware of his presence, laying a trap for me. But like I said. I know your moves."

The Monster trio and Granny battered and bruised, Liam addressed the thug testing the Hyde formula. "How's it look, mate?"

"Another few minutes. The formula is complicated. Like nothing I've ever seen."

"No," Liam said. "I would think not."

Barely up on her knees, Agatha held her sickened gut. She was learning the depth and breadth of her Beast strengths—and weaknesses—in real-time.

"What can you alone do with the formula? You're just one man. You know we'd find you, sooner or later."

"Why do you think?" Liam said incredulously.

"For your bluh… bloody birthright! For the power!"

"Of course, for the bloody power, you stupid cow! For the *unbelievable* power. Enough to change the fate of the world. And, to be more precise," Liam said, lording over Agatha now, "to save it."

"Save it? From whom?"

"Who else you, you twit? From MI7. The Dame School. From all of *you*!"

"From me?" Agatha said. "What did I do?"

"It's not what you've done, dear cousin. But what you will do… and why."

"I… I don't understand."

"Because deep at its core, Dame is like every other school. They claim to educate you, to teach you to… expand your mind. But all they really do is shut down your thoughts. They keep you so distracted with training and mission protocols and *their* version of who they see as being noble and shite, that they never tell you the bloody truth."

Kill him, Blythe demanded. *You're wasting time. KILL HIM!*

Agatha refused to relent, but it was getting more difficult to fight off Blythe. "What truth?"

"Don't listen to him," Lily said. "He's a nutter, full stop. It's why they kicked him out. You remember what he was like. Full of conspiracy theories and shadow governments and the game behind the bloody game. Anything to make himself feel smarter and more important than everyone else."

"And you don't?" Liam decried. "Look around the world. The age of the dictator is on the rise once more. Racists, bigots, and neo-Nazis are stronger than they've been in decades. Overpopulation? Technology? The rich gouging the poor? The world is changing so fast that we can't even pretend to keep up. Russia. China, North Korea. Transylvania. The Middle East. You think it's all a nuisance, but the dominoes are falling. And the key to it all… is The Ten."

"The Ten?" Agatha said. "What's The Ten?"

"Oh," Liam chuffed with delighted arrogance. "Granny never told you, did she? Mr. Snow, either?" His smile stretched ear to ear. "Why am I not surprised."

"Don't," Granny mumbled. "They're not… they're not ready."

"What does being ready have to do with reality?" Liam said. "You've coddled them for too long. And look at the price. You put a claim on virtue. But really… who's the villain now?"

Agatha turned to Granny who, despite being anesthetized, revealed a depth of worry and sorrow on her face Agatha had never seen before.

"Gran. Who are The… Ten?" But Agatha knew, without really knowing. She'd heard the rumors, whispers in the hall. But this was the first time anyone had spoken of The Ten out in the open.

"They're Monsters," Gilbert wheezed. "Scattered throughout the world. Political and religious leaders. CEOs. Private military contractors. Heads of nonprofits. Entertainers. Social media influencers. Technologists. They have power and penetration. It's seeped in."

Liam was impressed. "Oooh, very good, Gilbert. Invisibility and brains. I didn't think you had it in you. But then again, being invisible does grant you access to all sorts of nasty little secrets, doesn't it?"

"I heard Mr. Snow talk about them," Gilbert said. "I snuck into his office, just looking around. But he came in with two other professors. Sai Ahuja, you know… that weretiger? And Isla Wilson, that mad Aussie scientist. They said The Ten had to be neutralized, or the world would go black. Only… their leadership is too high-profile to take down in typical fashion. MI7 needed a new plan."

"Why didn't you tell us?" Agatha said. "You never said a bloody word."

"It was," Gilbert stammered with his visible bloody lip. "I don't know. It was just… too much to think about. I was still trying to figure out just how to be"—he shrugged invisibly— "me."

"And while Mr. Snow and the other Dame School tossers were fretting about what to do, they did, as usual, cock the whole thing up," Liam said. "By wasting time, paralysis by analysis. Training you twits for silly little missions that mean sod all."

"The Dame School isn't meant for those kinds of

missions," Agatha said.

Liam snarled, leaning so close to Agatha she could almost feel his trembling muscles.

"Well, they bloody well should be! Look at the Yanks. They thought Obama was the turning point of a new progressive world. But it was all delusion. The only thing they actually accomplished was to rub his ascension in the face of those who loathed his very existence. And then Harris as a desperate move, clinging to an idea that had already expired. And as we predicted, a delusional puppet rose in America, inserted by The Ten, to wage a culture and economic war that will stretch across the globe. Nothing like some good ole ethnic and political cleansing… demonizing immigrants, queers, and the poor, and Bob's your uncle. Democracy has never been all that democratic. And it's about to get worse. Little by little, day by day, you'll see America tear itself apart. The same happening the world over. As America flows, the rest of us bloody follow. We're fighting the wrong enemies. And in the process, we're creating new ones. The Ten is at the heart of it all. This madness must end, or it will be the end of *us*."

Agatha kept pushing. "The world has always been filled with shady deeds, greedy wankers, and hateful twats. But you've gone mad. What's this got to do with the formula?"

Liam laughed in a way that let them all know he had, perhaps, actually lost his mind.

Before Agatha could test him further, Liam's White Mask associate approached with the vial of bubbling red elixir. "Confirmed," he said. "It's authentic."

Liam took the vial between his thumb and forefinger like it was the holy grail itself. The elixir turned purple. He opened the vial, met with an eruption of escaped vapor. Liam inhaled the acrid solution, closed his eyes, and exhaled. He held the formula close.

"Finally," he said. "You've come home."

"Liam," Agatha pleaded. "If you're right... if there really is a cult of personality ruling the world from underground... if The Ten are as powerful as you say... what will the formula really do for you?"

"You don't see it, do you?" He raised the formula toward his lips. "Lazy, hateful sheep—mobs—hiding in packs to justify their ugliness. They're disparate now. But soon... they will have a global army. We have to fight them at every level, in every way, every bloody day, or we will find ourselves enslaved by a new age of darkness. We have to infiltrate The Ten. There is no other mission worthy of our attention. They will become monsters. And as you well know, the only way to fight a monster is to *be a Monster*."

"You still haven't answered my question," Agatha said, regaining her strength, testing Liam. "Why is the formula so—?"

Liam glared. "You think you're the HEROES? You're the bloody PROBLEM! You're so busy with trade embargoes and terror cells and self-righteous indignation you don't see they're the least of our worries. NONE of you see! Because it's a problem you can't solve with your cloak and dagger. The problems we face—The Ten—are bigger than us all. And none of you are willing to accept just how far into the heart of darkness we've already traveled. But now," he said and brought the formula to his lips, "I can finally do something about it."

With the satisfaction that can only come from possessing what one most desires, Liam drank the Hyde formula, transforming him into a Monster. And in his case, a Beast.

Planning her next move, Agatha examined the room, praying Granny would survive and that the formula would, in fact, kill Liam. She didn't want to consider how his inner Beast would manifest. Blythe giggled in her mind.

Liam is my kinda bloke. Time to let me play.

The White Mask thug closest to Lily began to gurgle, choking on his blood splatter. His own knife was wedged into his brain stem.

From behind him emerged the bloody, floating face that was Gilbert. In quick succession, the Invisible retracted the knife, reached around, and stole the White Mask's shotgun. As if the weapon floated in mid-air, it seemed to fire under its own power. With cold-blooded precision, Gilbert shot the other two White Masks in the chest with the elephant tranq, killing them both.

Left alive was team Agatha... and Liam, now a full-on Beast.

Seizing the opportunity, Gilbert fired the shotgun at him too. But the barrel was empty.

"That won't work on me now," said Liam, who in Beast form stood nearly seven feet tall. He studied his massive torso, admiring his enormity. He pumped his fists as he breathed deeply, the Hyde formula fusing within his cells. "I dreamed on this power for so long… but I never realized it would be so wonderfully"—he inhaled once more, allowing the oxygen to penetrate more deeply into his Beast lungs, then exhaled—"intoxicating."

Agatha saw the shift in Liam's eyes. His human personality was no longer in control. But as Agatha had already learned with dire consequences, the inner struggle was not to be taken lightly, and not easily maneuvered. Which presented an opportunity.

"Who am I talking to?" Agatha said. In a pre-arranged code, she tapped the floor with her pointer finger three times, alerting her team that she was buying them time to refine their attack. "Because I know it's not Liam."

"Oh, you are good," he said. "I am Alastair. But unlike you, you pathetic fool, I am not in battle with my human half. Liam is more like me than you think. Just as your inner Beast is more like you."

Taking advantage of the moment, Gilbert slid the knife over to Lily, who jabbed it into the sternum of the White Mask thug on the floor.

Gilbert dove next to him so that his demonic visage— he'd deliberately smeared the blood over his invisible face, giving him definition—was in Alastair's sightline, tempting his bloodlust.

Despite her broken foot, Lily cheetah-flipped through the air with tactical brilliance, away from Alastair, who shifted his enormous body toward her.

Choreographed as the team had practiced—Liam

now in position—Agatha morphed back into her Beast self, raising both gargantuan arms above her head.

With visions of the Liam she once knew and the unworthy teenage crush she'd foolishly had on him, Agatha gripped her Monster hands together and, with angst, humiliation, vengeance, and unfiltered Monster rage, forged them into one incredible hammer.

And like one does with any tool such as hers, she came down upon Alastair with the force of a dozen wrecking balls.

It was Gilbert, however, who utilized their captor's efforts against them. Unbeknownst to Alastair, Gilbert had shackled his Monster feet together with a large White Mask zip-tie, enough to disrupt his balance, toppling Alastair as Agatha bashed his face.

The two Monsters crashed to the floor, wailing on each other, blow after mighty blow. In their struggle, Alastair snapped the zip-tie apart. He popped up on his feet, lifted Agatha over his head, and, with incomprehensible thrust and violence, heaved his Monster combatant against the wall.

"Your team is nothing." About to pummel his Monster foe, Alastair felt woozy, as if he'd been drugged. His Monster strength suddenly and unexpectedly began to wane. "You are a failure in every way that matters."

Kill him! Blythe demanded. *Kill him NOW!*

Though stunned, Agatha was back on her feet, unwilling to set Blythe loose. Although the temptation was fierce.

"You're the only failure I see." She charged at Alastair

like a taunted buffalo, then slammed him back to the floor. The entire room shook. "You invent conspiracies to justify your paranoia. You're a junkie and a pervert like any other, and your *kink*… is power."

Locked in savage battle, Agatha stared into Alastair's eyes. She realized that her mishandling of the Hyde formula had not just given them both remarkable strength and ruthlessness. She had unleashed mighty hellhounds upon the Earth.

"You still don't get it," Alastair said as they literally pushed back on each other. Counterbalanced by Monster hands on Monster shoulders, Monster feet dug into the helpless floor, ripping up the concrete like tractors excavating farmland. Alastair was losing his balance and leverage, his strength continuing to drain. "You think I'm the enemy, when in truth, I'm your savior. I'm your white knight with a righteous mask. I'm the only one with the knowledge, might, and will to topple those who enslave us. To topple The Ten. But if you won't deal with reality, then deal with this. Once I've killed you and your team, Granny is next."

Accepting the Liam she knew was truly gone, if she had ever truly known him, Agatha unlocked the deepest layer of savagery in her own conflicted soul.

"No! I may be a Monster. But I will always and forever… be a Jekyll. And that means I will never give in," she said, addressing Alastair—and Blythe. Her massive, outstretched arms pushed on Alastair's shoulders, as he pushed on hers. "Not now. Not ever. Stop this, Alastair. Or you"—with her Monster hands she smashed his Monster face, a blow that buckled his hulking knees—"will"—she bashed him once more, Alastair's inner resolve giving way—"die!"

With one final, thunderous blow to his head, Alastair went down.

Broken. Battered. Lost.

"W-why... is this happening to me," Liam mewled, his Monster strength nearly gone, reduced to his human form. "Where is my... power?"

"Because you *are* the three percent," Lily said. "You wouldn't face *your* reality, so we used it against you. Your arrogance and insatiable need to rule were always your downfall. We tried to warn you. You wouldn't listen."

"It doesn't"—Liam huffed, his body beginning to melt inside and out—"matter. We tuh-took Granny's blood. It may take months, years, or even decades. But eventually we will distill the Hyde formula. We will control it once and for all. And then," he said, his gooey eyes rolling back into his deformed head, "we will be free of MI7... and take the battle to The Ten. And yuh... you will have wasted your lives in the meantime, fighting battles you've been told are important, but in the end, don't matter at all."

Agatha reduced herself back to her human size and form. "Who is *we*? Only Jekylls can take..." Like a drowned corpse, the bloated truth rose to the surface of her mind. There was no point in fighting it any longer. She finally acknowledge to herself what she'd always known, as much as she did not want to know it.

"There are more of us from the bloodline out there,

ready to battle The Ten," Liam said, nearly hissing. "Taken at birth, hidden from Dame, so we don't waste what precious tuh… time we have left. We will amass an army, dear cousin. We Hydes. And when that day comes, if you do not accept what you know in your heart is true, then you and all those you luh… love, will be our enemies too. And if that happens, we will destroy you. Your link to the family bloodline will be severed. Forever."

Agatha and her conflicted psyche could take no more. Immediately morphing back into the Beast, she stepped aside within the battleground of her mind.

Released at last, Blythe reacted with inconsolable rampage.

"Now," she snarled, surging with violent, erotic compulsion, "Blythe can feed. Blythe can crush and Blythe"—a malevolent smile emerged—"can *kill.*"

With one Monster hand, Blythe grabbed the liquifying Liam by the throat, dangling him and his human form over the floor. With her other Monster hand, Blythe gripped his tiny, human skull, her Monster claws dug in, about to tear his head clean off his tiny human shoulders.

"Agatha!" commanded a now-alert Granny, who Lily had cut out of the explosive collar. Unshackled, Granny wielded the very same tranq gun that had put her down. "Stop this. Now. I know the unquenchable thirst for violence. Blythe is a part of you, but not the best of you. You have to regain control."

"NO!" Blythe roared. "I will never go back. Blythe is here. Blythe is free. And now that I am, this body… this power… is MINE!"

"AGATHA! I may be Granny to you, but I am also Jocasta."

Granny morphed into her own Beast. The transformation stunned Blythe who, despite her demands to remain in control, was startled—and terrified. Neither Agatha nor Blythe had ever seen Granny in Monster form.

If the creature standing before her was Granny's inner Monster—not just a physical transformation into a brutal, deformed Beast, but a psychological savage without a trace of humanity—then Agatha was no better. And possibly, even worse.

Jocasta was a reflection of Blythe and what Agatha had unleashed upon herself—and the world. If Jocasta was the worst of what Granny could become, then what would that mean for Agatha?

But as an experienced warrior trained in the Monster arts, Granny exerted her dominance over Jocasta, morphing back into human form.

"Agatha," Granny said. "I know you're in there. I know you can hear me. Liam's death is inevitable. He lied to you on the video. He wanted you to think he'd broken me. He didn't. I would *never* give him anything to hurt you. Ever. But if you kill him, you will be guilty. Of murder. A selfish act of vengeance to satisfy your bloodlust. If you fall prey to your worst Hyde instincts—which is what he's counting on—you will have already lost."

"But I *have* lost already," Agatha snarled, fighting through Blythe's influence. "So much. Too much."

Not to be denied, Blythe re-asserted herself. "Because of him and his *lies!*" With a Monster hand, she dangled

Liam like a diseased possum. "I must snap his neck! To kill him!"

Granny held her ground. "Resist, Agatha Lynn. Your parents didn't give their lives to see you fall. *This* is why we wait to take the formula. One must understand its power before merging with it. The surge is extraordinary."

Twisted up inside, Agatha howled in existential pain. The brutal cry reverberated in the dark basement, littered with broken bodies, torn flesh—and blood she would never be able to wash off.

As Liam literally dangled from her clawed hand, she saw her friends and Granny staring at her, horrified at what she'd become.

Who cares what they think? Blythe whispered. *Monster? Beast? They're nothing but words. We* have *strength. We* have *power. If Liam's going to die anyway, then let's have some fun.*

"Damn you!" Agatha howled, tormented by all the voices pulling on her soul. There may have been a way through the jungle in her mind. But rather than cut through the vines of logic, she squeezed Liam's neck tighter, about to crush his trachea, silencing him before he could twist her up with yet another lie. Or a truth she refused to hear. She had been pushed to the brink of her most savage self. And someone had to pay. "Damn you all to—"

Four massive blasts rattled their ears.

Agatha lurched forward, feeling the dense metal slugs pierce her back. The individual shots were not enough to take her down, but each one of them hurt. Wounding her body—and her pride.

With madness behind her Beast eyes, black and red, she turned to see a tranq gun hovering in the air, with Gil's bloody face looking up at her. He pumped her full of the rhino tranq.

"I've learned we all have truths that are invisible to us," he said. "And I won't let *yours*… destroy *you*."

Before she could respond, Agatha felt another tranq blast to the leg, this one from Lily.

"I'm sorry," the Cheetah said.

Spun around, Agatha took another tranq to the chest.

"Granny?" Agatha whimpered, faltering, down on one knee. "But you..."

Granny pumped the tranq gun and unloaded two more blasts to Agatha's chest. "You can hate me all you want," she said, "but if *his* blood isn't on *your* hands, it will all have been worth it."

So enraged was Agatha, caught between the two personalities battling for control of her soul, that she could neither see nor accept that the assault on her was not a brutal attack, but an act of love. Tranq-style. Agatha dropped Liam to the floor and, no longer able or willing to distinguish between friend and foe, charged at Granny.

Encircled by familiar faces, Agatha was bombarded by gun blasts, one tranq after another until, finally, her raging Beast body, howling with Beast fury and teenaged hormonal rage, could take no more.

Like Han Solo frozen in carbonite, with a mighty *whomp* Agatha went down face first on the concrete floor. Her last vision was of Liam, whose own life force was about to leave him.

"I'm suh-sorry," he whispered, dissolving into a puddle, "but the war has already begun."

It wasn't lost on Agatha, as she morphed into human form, that the conflict he meant was the war within herself.

9

Days later, back at the Dame School, Agatha was called into Mr. Snow's office. Lily, Gilbert, and Granny were already present, seated around his desk.

"How are you feeling?" the Yeti said.

"A little sore, but alright."

"Good. You'll need your strength. We have a lot to talk about."

"The Ten?" Agatha rubbed Granny's shoulder. Granny smiled back. "And Granny having the formula?"

"Yes," Mr. Snow said. "The Ten. And we overlooked the other matter."

"Because going against me would expose MI7." Granny had an edge in her voice. "I didn't survive this long by being stupid."

"Mr. Snow," Agatha said. "Liam… before he died… said there are Hydes out there too. Members of the Hyde bloodline taking the Hyde formula. He said they're more deadly even than… well… me. Us. Jekylls, I mean. Is that true?"

Slow to answer, the Yeti exchanged a subtle glance with Granny. "A conversation for another day. But I'd not put much faith in what Liam said. His truths, as usual, were entangled with lies."

In full Dame School gear, Gilbert leaned forward invisibly in his chair. "But was Liam right? About The Ten?"

"I would very much like to tell you that Liam was wrong in this case, but in truth, yes… I'm afraid he was right. The Ten are on the rise. It is our mission to stop them."

"How do we do that?" said Lily who, broken foot on the mend, had asked a question on all their minds.

"By training you full-stop," Mr. Snow said. "Your probationary status is over."

Agatha had spent the last few days in bed, coming to an agreement with Blythe. There was no getting past that Blythe was a part of Agatha, as much as Agatha was a part of Blythe. They were going to have to find a way to co-exist, or else they would, sooner or later, destroy each other. And if not, be destroyed by something—or someone—far worse.

She also acknowledged how far Liam had fallen in his unquenchable lust for the Hyde power and validation of his ego. And how easily she could be tempted to seek the same fate.

Would Blythe ever take over and pull her completely into the darkness? Perhaps. But that was the benefit of having a team around her. Even at her worst… especially at her worst… they would always have her back.

"Then let's get bloody started," Agatha said. "Because if The Ten are as dangerous as you say, we don't have a minute to lose."

About the Author

Russ Colchamiro is author of the Sci-Fi thrillers *Crackle and Fire, Fractured Lives, Hot Ash, Blunt Force Rising,* and *Trigger Point,* the ongoing series featuring hardboiled private eye Angela Hardwicke. Russ is also the author of the rollicking time travel/space adventure, *Crossline,* is the editor of the Sci-Fi mystery anthology *Love, Murder & Mayhem,* co-author and co-editor of the noir anthology *Murder in Montague Falls* and has contributed to various other anthologies.

A member of The Mystery Writers Association, The Private Eye Writers of America, Horror Writers Association, and author collective Crazy 8 Press, Russ also hosts and produces his Russ's Rockin' Rollercoaster podcast, where he interviews best-selling and up-and-coming Sci-Fi, fantasy, crime, mystery, thriller, and horror authors.

He lives in New Jersey with his wife, twin ninjas, black lab, Jinx, and precocious cat, Callie.

Social Media:
Web site: russcolchamiro.com
Instagram, Threads: @AuthorDudeRuss
Blue Sky: @AuthorDudeRuss.bsky.social
YouTube: https://www.youtube.com/@authorduderuss/featured
Facebook: https://www.facebook.com/russ.colchamiro

DOWN THESE MEANS STREETS
of Magic & Monsters walk the

MYSTIC INVESTIGATORS

THE WILDSIDHE
OMNIBUS
CHRONICLES • VOL. 1-6
No teachers. No parents.
School is out...of this world!
PATRICK THOMAS • JUDITH TRACY
TONY DIGEROLAMO • MYKE COLE

Even the teenage Queen of Darkness needs a friend
A NYX & SHIVERS BOOK
EMOTIONAL SUPPORT
NIGHTMARE
PATRICK T. FIBBS

One Last Chance to Save
Happily Ever After

Can a group of heroes including Goldenhair, Red Riding Hood and Rapunzel help General Snow White and her dwarven resistance fighters defeat the tyrannical Queen Cinderella? And will they succeed before a war with Wonderland destroys everything?

Their only hope to stop Cinderella's quest for power lies with a young girl named Patience Muffet who carries the fabled shards of Cinderella's glass slippers.

Roy Mauritsen's fantasy adventure fairy tale epic begins with *Shards Of The Glass Slipper: Queen Cinder.*

**"Fantastic...
A Magnificent Epic!**
-*Sarah Beth Durst* author of
Into The Wild & Drink, Slay, Love

**"The Brothers Grimm
meets
Lord Of The Rings!"**
-*Patrick Thomas*, author
of the Murphy's Lore series

"Shards is a dark, lush, full-throttle fantasy epic that presents a bold re-imagining of classic characters."
-David Wade, creator of
319 Dark Street

"Roy Mauritsen's enchanting epic comes at a time when fairy tales are back in the forefront of our collective imagination."
-Darin Kennedy,
short fiction author

PADWOLF PUBLISHING

In paperback & e-book
Find out more at:
shardsoftheglassslipper.com
padwolf.com

Bikini Jones

Being *CURSED* to wear a bikini
Won't stop this Hero
From *SAVING* the world

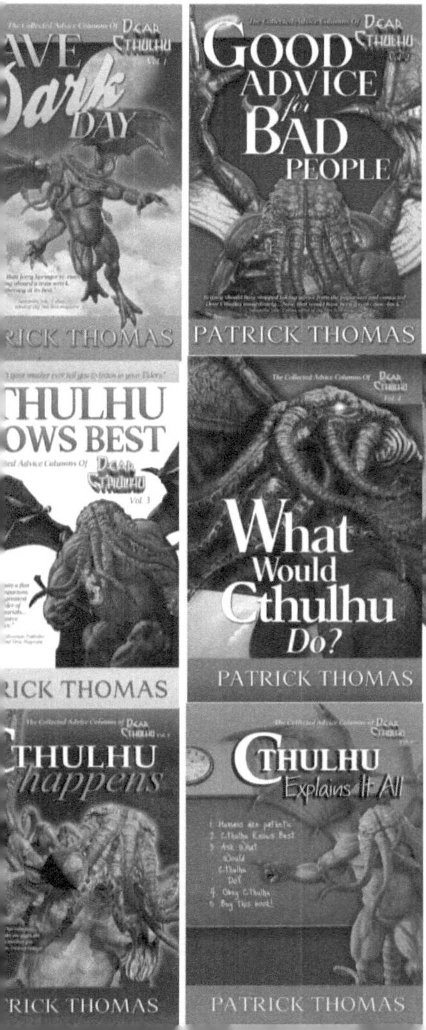

Dear Cthulhu

THE ADVICE
COLUMN TO
***END* ALL**
ADVICE COLUMNS

www.ingramcontent.com/pod-product-compliance
Lightning Source LLC
Chambersburg PA
CBHW021722190726
48289CB00008B/2655